CLASSIC NURSERY RHYMES

THIS BOOK
BELONGS
TO

_____

_____

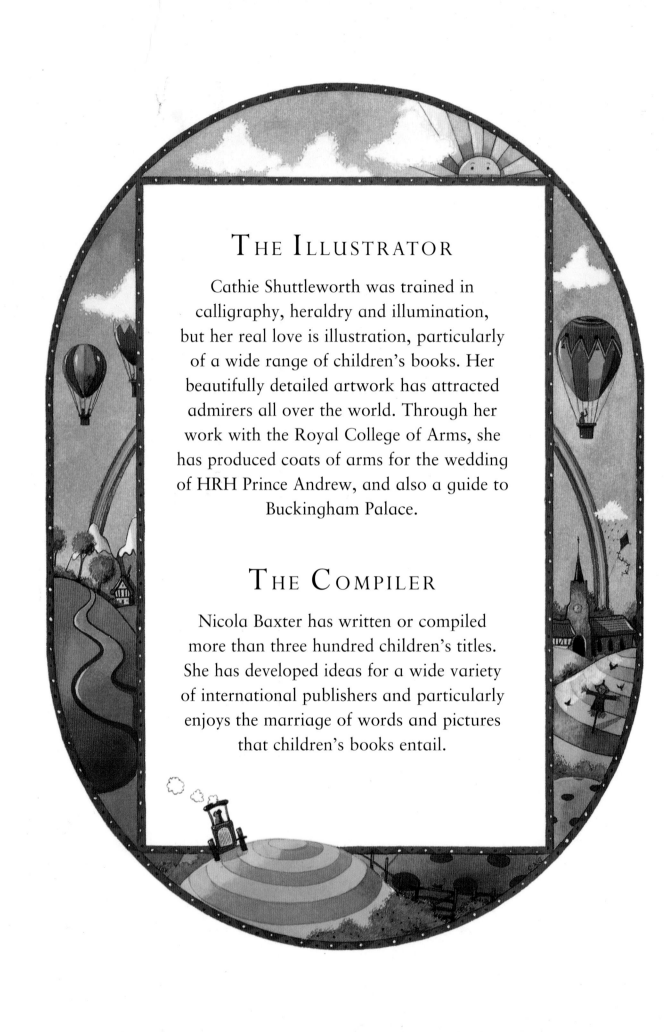

THE ILLUSTRATOR

Cathie Shuttleworth was trained in calligraphy, heraldry and illumination, but her real love is illustration, particularly of a wide range of children's books. Her beautifully detailed artwork has attracted admirers all over the world. Through her work with the Royal College of Arms, she has produced coats of arms for the wedding of HRH Prince Andrew, and also a guide to Buckingham Palace.

THE COMPILER

Nicola Baxter has written or compiled more than three hundred children's titles. She has developed ideas for a wide variety of international publishers and particularly enjoys the marriage of words and pictures that children's books entail.

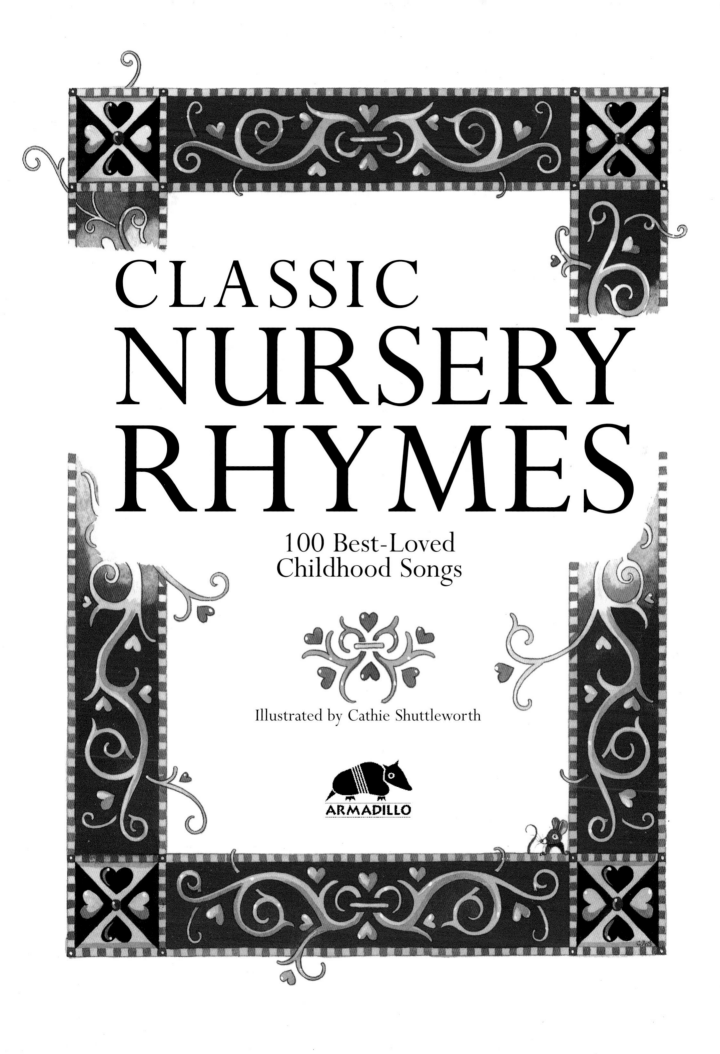

CLASSIC
NURSERY
RHYMES

100 Best-Loved
Childhood Songs

Illustrated by Cathie Shuttleworth

ARMADILLO

FOR MY SISTER DORA – C.A.S.

This edition is published by Armadillo, an imprint of Anness Publishing Ltd,
Blaby Road, Wigston, Leicestershire LE18 4SE; info@anness.com

www.annesspublishing.com

If you like the images in this book and would like to investigate using them
for publishing, promotions or advertising, please visit our website
www.practicalpictures.com for more information.

Publisher: Joanna Lorenz
Produced by Nicola Baxter
Designer: Amanda Hawkes
Production Controller: Don Campaniello

PUBLISHER'S NOTE
Although the information in this book is believed to be accurate and true at
the time of going to press, neither the authors nor the publisher can accept
any legal responsibility or liability for any errors or omissions
that may have been made.

Manufacturer: Anness Publishing Ltd, Blaby Road, Wigston,
Leicestershire LE18 4SE, England
For Product Tracking go to: www.annesspublishing.com/tracking
Batch: 6052-20928-1127

CONTENTS

ABOUT NURSERY RHYMES

Children love the rhythm and repetition
of nursery rhymes. Babies fall asleep to
rocking and singing. Later, toddlers join in
with the words and actions themselves.
Later still, rhymes are part of playground
games. The origins of many nursery
rhymes are lost in time, but their future
is safe with each new generation.

Hickory, dickory, dock,
The mice ran up the clock...
And over these pages,
You'll seek them for ages,
Hickory, dickory, dock.

ANIMAL RHYMES

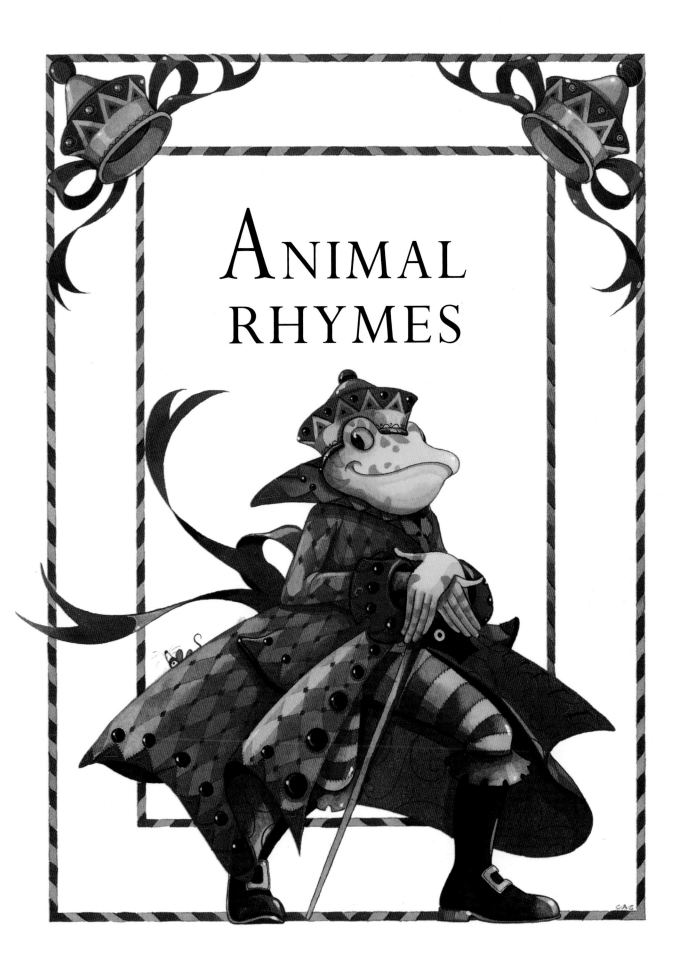

Old Mother Goose,
When she wanted to wander,
Would ride through the air
On a very fine gander.

Mother Goose had a house,
'Twas built in a wood,
An owl at the door
For a porter stood.

She had a son Jack,
A plain-looking lad,
He was not very good,
Nor yet very bad.

She sent him to market,
A live goose he bought:
"Here! Mother," says he,
"It will not go for naught."

Jack's goose and her gander
Grew very fond;
They'd both eat together,
Or swim in one pond.

Jack found one morning,
As I have been told,
His goose had laid him
An egg of pure gold.

Jack rode to his mother,
The news for to tell.
She called him a good boy,
And said it was well.

Higgledy, piggledy, my black hen,
She lays eggs for gentlemen;
Gentlemen come every day
To see what my black hen doth lay.
Sometimes nine and sometimes ten,
She lays eggs for gentlemen.

Goosey, goosey, gander,
Whither shall I wander?
Upstairs, downstairs,
And in my lady's chamber.

There I met an old man,
Who wouldn't say his prayers.
I took him by the left leg
And threw him down the stairs.

10

Cock-a-doodle-doo!
My dame has lost her shoe!
My master's lost his fiddling stick
And doesn't know what to do!

Cock-a-doodle-doo!
What is my dame to do?
Till master finds his fiddling stick,
She'll dance without her shoe!

Cock-a-doodle-doo!
My dame has found her shoe.
And master's found his fiddling stick,
Sing doodle-doodle-doo!

Cock-a-doodle-doo!
My dame will dance with you.
While master fiddles his fiddling stick
For dame and doodle-doo.

Ride a cock-horse to Banbury Cross
To see a fine lady
        upon a white horse.
With rings on her fingers
And bells on her toes,
She shall have music
        wherever she goes!

This is the way the ladies ride,
Nimble, nimble, nimble, nimble.
This is the way the gentlemen ride,
A gallop, a trot, a gallop, a trot.
This is the way the farmers ride,
Jiggety-jog, jiggety-jog.
And when they come to a hedge,
They jump over!
And when they come to
        a slippery space,
They scramble, scramble, scramble,
Tumble-down Dick!

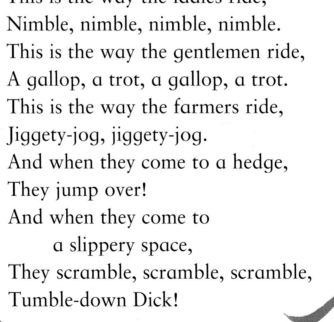

Yankee Doodle went to town,
Riding on a pony;
He stuck a feather in his cap
And called it macaroni.

I had a little pony,
His name was Dapple Grey;
I lent him to a lady,
To ride a mile away.
She whipped him,
She slashed him,
She rode him through the mire;
I would not lend my pony now,
For all the lady's hire.

One white foot, buy him.
Two white feet, try him.
Three white feet, wait and see.
Four white feet, let him be.

Hickory, dickory, dock,
The mouse ran up the clock.
The clock struck one,
The mouse ran down,
Hickory, dickory, dock.

Six little mice sat down to spin;
Pussy passed by, and she peeped in.
What are you doing, my little men?
Weaving coats for gentlemen.
Shall I come in
And cut off your threads?
No, no, Mistress Pussy,
You'd bite off our heads.
Oh no, I won't,
I'll help you spin.
That may be so,
But you can't come in!

14

Three blind mice,
See how they run!
They all ran after the farmer's wife,
Who cut off their tails with a
     carving knife,
Did ever you see such a sight in
     your life,
As three blind mice?

Little Tommy Tittlemouse
Lived in a little house;
He caught fishes
In other men's ditches.

Pussy cat, pussy cat,
Where have you been?
I've been up to London
To look at the Queen.
Pussy cat, pussy cat,
What did you there?
I frightened a little mouse
Under her chair.

15

The north wind doth blow,
And we shall have snow,
And what will poor robin do then,
Poor thing?

He'll sit in a barn,
And keep himself warm,
And hide his head under his wing,
Poor thing.

A wise old owl lived in an oak;
The more he saw, the less he spoke;
The less he spoke, the more he heard.
Why can't we all be
Like that wise old bird?

16

Two little birds sat on a wall,
One named Peter,
One named Paul.
Fly away, Peter!
Fly away, Paul!
Come back, Peter!
Come back, Paul!

There were two crows sat on a stone,
One flew away and there was one.
The other, seeing his partner gone,
He flew away and there were none.

Three little kittens
They lost their mittens
And they began to cry,
Oh mother dear, we sadly fear
That we have lost our mittens.
What! Lost your mittens,
You naughty kittens?
Then you shall have no pie.
Mee-ow, mee-ow, mee-ow,
No, you shall have no pie.

The three little kittens
They found their mittens
And they began to cry,
Oh mother dear, see here, see here,
For we have found our mittens.
Put on your mittens,
You silly kittens,
And you shall have some pie.
Purr-r, purr-r, purr-r,
Oh, let us have some pie.

The three little kittens
Put on their mittens
And soon ate up the pie.
Oh mother dear, we greatly fear
That we have soiled our mittens.
What! Soiled your mittens,
You naughty kittens?
Then they began to sigh,
Mee-ow, mee-ow, mee-ow,
Then they began to sigh.

The three little kittens
They washed their mittens
And hung them out to dry.
Oh! Mother dear, do you not hear
That we have washed our mittens?
What! Washed your mittens,
You good little kittens?
But I smell a rat close by.
Mee-ow, mee-ow, mee-ow,
We smell a rat close by.

19

A cat came fiddling out of a barn,
With a pair of bagpipes
Under her arm;
She could sing nothing
But "Fiddle-de-dee,
The mouse has married
The bumble bee."
Pipe, cat; dance, mouse;
We'll have a wedding
At our good house.

I love little pussy,
Her coat is so warm,
And if I don't hurt her,
She'll do me no harm.
So I'll not pull her tail,
Nor drive her away,
But pussy and I
Very gently will play.

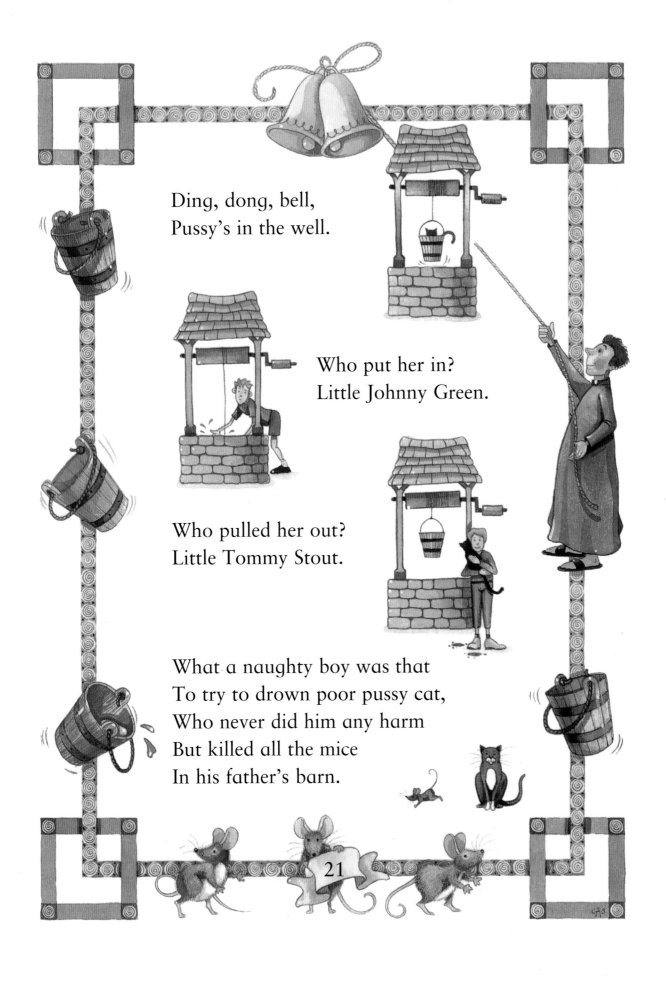

Ding, dong, bell,
Pussy's in the well.

Who put her in?
Little Johnny Green.

Who pulled her out?
Little Tommy Stout.

What a naughty boy was that
To try to drown poor pussy cat,
Who never did him any harm
But killed all the mice
In his father's barn.

I saw a ship a-sailing,
A-sailing on the sea,
And oh, but it was laden
With pretty things for thee!

There were comfits in the cabin
And apples in the hold;
The sails were made of silk
And the masts were all of gold!

The four and twenty sailors
Who stood between the decks
Were four and twenty white mice
With chains about their necks.

The captain was a duck
With a packet on his back,
And when the ship began to move,
The captain said, "Quack! Quack!"

Cackle, cackle, Mother Goose,
Have you any feathers loose?
Truly have I, pretty fellow,
Half enough to fill a pillow.
Here are quills,
Take one or two,
And down to make
A bed for you.

Baa, baa, black sheep,
Have you any wool?
Yes, sir, yes, sir,
Three bags full.
One for my master,
And one for my dame,
And one for the little boy
Who lives down the lane.

23

Mary had a little lamb,
    Its fleece was white as snow;
And everywhere that Mary went,
    The lamb was sure to go.

It followed her to school one day,
    That was against the rule;
It made the children laugh and play
    To see a lamb at school.

And so the teacher turned it out,
    But still it lingered near;
And waited patiently about,
    Till Mary did appear.

"Why does the lamb love Mary so?"
    The eager children cry;
"Why, Mary loves the lamb, you know,"
    The teacher did reply.

NURSERY RHYME PEOPLE

There was an old woman
      who lived in a shoe,
She had so many children
      she didn't know what to do.
She gave them some broth
      without any bread,
And scolded them soundly
      and sent them to bed.

26

Girls and boys, come out to play,
The moon doth shine as bright as day.
Leave your supper and leave your sleep,
And come with your playfellows into
     the street.
          Come with a whoop,
          And come with a call,
          Come with a good will,
          Or come not at all.
Up the ladder and down the wall,
A half-penny loaf will serve us all;
You find milk, and I'll find flour,
And we'll have a pudding in
     half an hour.

Sing a song of sixpence,
A pocket full of rye;
Four and twenty blackbirds,
Baked in a pie.

When the pie was opened,
The birds began to sing;
Wasn't that a dainty dish
To set before a King?

The King was in his counting house,
Counting out his money;
The Queen was in the parlour
Eating bread and honey.

The maid was in the garden,
Hanging out the clothes,
When down came a blackbird,
And pecked off her nose!

28

Humpty Dumpty sat on a wall,
Humpty Dumpty had a great fall.
All the King's horses
And all the King's men
Couldn't put Humpty together again.

Rub-a-dub-dub,
Three men in a tub,
And how do you think they got there?
The butcher, the baker,
The candlestick-maker,
They all jumped out of a rotten potato.
'Twas enough to make a man stare!

29

Jack and Jill went up the hill,
To fetch a pail of water;
Jack fell down and broke his crown,
And Jill came tumbling after.

Up Jack got and home did trot,
As fast as he could caper,
He went to bed and mended his head,
With vinegar and brown paper.

30

Solomon Grundy,
Born on Monday,
Christened on Tuesday,
Married on Wednesday,
Took ill on Thursday,
Worse on Friday,
Died on Saturday,
Buried on Sunday,
And that was the end
Of Solomon Grundy.

Monday's child is fair of face,
Tuesday's child is full of grace,
Wednesday's child is full of woe,
Thursday's child has far to go,
Friday's child is loving and giving,
Saturday's child works hard for a living,
But the child that is born on the
                    Sabbath day
Is bonny and blithe, and good, and gay.

Polly, put the kettle on,
Polly, put the kettle on,
Polly, put the kettle on,
We'll all have tea.

Sukey, take it off again,
Sukey, take it off again,
Sukey, take it off again,
They've all gone away.

Blow the fire and make the toast,
Put the muffins on to roast,
Who is going to eat the most?
We'll all have tea.

32

Simple Simon met a pieman
Going to the fair;
Said Simple Simon to the pieman,
"Let me taste your wares."

Said the pieman to Simple Simon,
"Show me first your penny."
Said Simple Simon to the pieman,
"Indeed, I haven't any."

Simple Simon went a-fishing,
For to catch a whale;
All the water he had got
Was in his mother's pail.

Simple Simon went to look
If plums grew on a thistle;
He pricked his finger very much,
Which made poor Simon whistle.

Oh, dear, what can the matter be?
Dear, dear, what can the matter be?
Oh, dear, what can the matter be?
Johnny's so long at the fair.

He promised to buy me
    a bunch of blue ribbons,
He promised to buy me
    a bunch of blue ribbons,
He promised to buy me
    a bunch of blue ribbons,
To tie up my bonny brown hair.

Where are you going to,
    my pretty maid?
I'm going a-milking, sir, she said.
May I come with you,
    my pretty maid?
Yes, if you like, kind sir, she said.
What is your fortune,
    my pretty maid?
My face is my fortune, sir, she said.
Then I cannot marry you,
    my pretty maid.
Nobody asked you, sir, she said.

Pretty maid, pretty maid,
Where have you been?
Gathering roses
To give to the Queen.
Pretty maid, pretty maid,
What gave she you?
She gave me a diamond
As big as my shoe.

35

There was a jolly miller once,
Lived on the river Dee;
He worked and sang
From morn till night,
No lark more blithe than he.
And this the burden of his song
Forever used to be:
I care for nobody, no, not I,
If nobody cares for me!

Blow, wind, blow! And go, mill, go!
That the miller may grind his corn;
That the baker may take it,
And into bread make it,
And bring us a loaf in the morn.

Old King Cole was a merry old soul,
And a merry old soul was he;
He called for his pipe,
And he called for his bowl,
And he called for his fiddlers three.

Every fiddler, he had a fine fiddle,
And a very fine fiddle had he;
Twee tweedle dee, tweedle dee, went
        the fiddlers.
Oh there's none so rare
As can compare
With King Cole and his fiddlers three.

Tweedledum and Tweedledee
Agreed to fight a battle,
For Tweedledum said Tweedledee
Had spoilt his nice new rattle.
Just then flew by a monstrous crow,
As black as a tar barrel,
Which frightened both the heroes so,
They quite forgot their battle.

Oh, the grand old Duke of York,
He had ten thousand men;
He marched them up to the top
        of the hill,
And he marched them down again.

And when they were up,
They were up,
And when they were down,
They were down,
And when they were only halfway up,
They were neither up nor down.

Peter, Peter, pumpkin eater,
Had a wife and couldn't keep her;
He put her in a pumpkin shell,
And there he kept her very well.
Peter, Peter, pumpkin eater,
Had another and didn't love her;
Peter learned to read and spell,
And then he loved her very well.

39

There was an old woman tossed up
    in a basket,
Seventeen times as high as the moon;
And where she was going, I couldn't
    but ask her,
For under her arm, she carried a
    broom.
Old woman, old woman, old woman,
    said I,
Whither, oh whither, oh whither so
    high?
To sweep the cobwebs out of the sky!
Shall I go with you?
Aye, by and by.

There was an old woman lived
    under a hill,
And if she's not gone, she's living
    there still.
Baked apples she sold, and cranberry
    pies,
And she's the old woman who never
    told lies.

Old Mother Hubbard
Went to the cupboard
To fetch her poor dog a bone.
But when she got there,
The cupboard was bare,
And so the poor dog had none.

She sent to the baker's
To buy him some bread;
But when she came back,
The poor dog was dead.

She went to the undertaker's
To buy him a coffin;
But when she came back,
The poor dog was laughing.

She took a clean dish
To get him some tripe;
But when she came back
He was smoking a pipe.

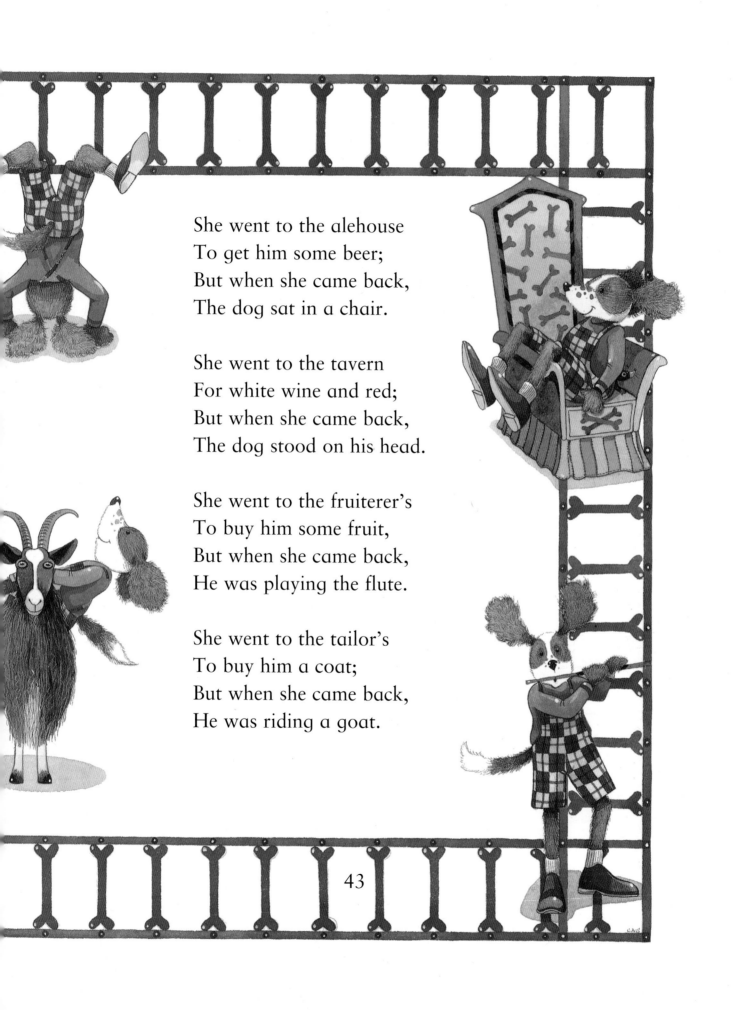

She went to the alehouse
To get him some beer;
But when she came back,
The dog sat in a chair.

She went to the tavern
For white wine and red;
But when she came back,
The dog stood on his head.

She went to the fruiterer's
To buy him some fruit,
But when she came back,
He was playing the flute.

She went to the tailor's
To buy him a coat;
But when she came back,
He was riding a goat.

She went to the hatter's
To buy him a hat;
But when she came back,
He was feeding the cat.

She went to the barber's
To buy him a wig;
But when she came back,
He was dancing a jig.

She went to the cobbler's
To buy him some shoes;
But when she came back,
He was reading the news.

She went to the seamstress
To buy him some linen;
But when she came back,
The dog was a-spinning.

44

She went to the hosier's
To buy him some hose;
But when she came back,
He was dressed in his clothes.

The dame made a curtsy,
The dog made a bow;
The dame said, "Your servant,"
The dog said, "Bow-wow."

45

Georgie Porgie,
Pudding and pie,
Kissed the girls
And made them cry.
When the boys
Came out to play,
Georgie Porgie
Ran away.

Little Jack Horner
Sat in a corner,
Eating his Christmas pie.
He put in his thumb,
And pulled out a plum,
And said, "What a good boy am I!"

Jack Sprat could eat no fat,
His wife could eat no lean,
And so between them both, you see,
They licked the platter clean.

Little Tommy Tucker
Sings for his supper;
What shall we give him?
Brown bread and butter.
How shall he cut it
Without a knife?
How will he be married
Without a wife?

Tom, Tom, the piper's son,
He learned to play when he was young,
And all the tune that he could play
Was "Over the hills and far away".
Over the hills and a great way off,
The wind shall blow my top-knot off.

Tom, Tom, the piper's son,
Stole a pig and away did run;
The pig was eat and Tom was beat,
And Tom went howling down the street.

Little Polly Flinders
Sat among the cinders,
Warming her pretty little toes;
Her mother came and caught her,
And whipped her little daughter
For spoiling her nice new clothes.

Lucy Locket lost her pocket,
Kitty Fisher found it.
Not a penny was there in it
But a ribbon round it.

Little Miss Muffet
Sat on a tuffet,
Eating her curds and whey.
Along came a spider,
Who sat down beside her,
And frightened Miss Muffet away.

See-saw, Margery Daw,
Jacky shall have a new master;
He shall have but a penny a day,
Because he can't work any faster!

49

It's raining, it's pouring,
The old man is snoring.
He went to bed
And bumped his head,
And couldn't get up in the morning!

Doctor Foster went to Gloucester
In a shower of rain;
He stepped in a puddle,
Right up to his middle,
And never went there again.

50

Peter Piper picked a peck of pickled
pepper;
A peck of pickled pepper Peter Piper
picked;
If Peter Piper picked a peck of
pickled pepper,
Where's the peck of pickled pepper
Peter Piper picked?

I do not like thee, Doctor Fell,
The reason why I cannot tell;
But this I know, I know right well,
I do not like thee, Doctor Fell.

Bobby Shafto's gone to sea,
Silver buckles on his knee;
He'll come back and marry me,
Bonny Bobby Shafto!

Bobby Shafto's fat and fair,
Combing down his yellow hair,
He's my love for ever more,
Bonny Bobby Shafto!

Little Boy Blue,
Come blow your horn,
The sheep's in the meadow,
The cow's in the corn.

Where is the boy
Who looks after the sheep?
He's under the haystack,
Fast asleep!

Will you wake him?
No, not I!
For if I do,
He's sure to cry.

53

Little Bo-Peep
Has lost her sheep,
And doesn't know where to find them.
Leave them alone,
And they'll come home,
Bringing their tails behind them.

Little Bo-Peep
Fell fast asleep,
And dreamed she heard them bleating.
But when she awoke,
She found it a joke,
For they were still a-fleeting.

Then up she took
Her little crook,
Determined for to find them.
She found them indeed,
But it made her heart bleed,
For they'd left their tails behind them.

It happened one day,
As Bo-Peep did stray
Into a meadow hard by,
There she espied
Their tails side by side,
All hung on a tree to dry.

She heaved a sigh,
And wiped her eye,
And over the hillocks went rambling,
And tried what she could,
As a shepherdess should,
To tack again each to its lambkin.

Little Bo-Peep
Has lost her sheep,
And doesn't know where to find them.
Leave them alone,
And they'll come home,
Bringing their tails behind them.

Lavender's blue, dilly, dilly,
Lavender's green;
When I am King, dilly, dilly,
You shall be Queen.

Call up your men, dilly, dilly,
Set them to work,
Some to the plough, dilly, dilly,
Some to the cart.

Some to make hay, dilly, dilly,
Some to thresh corn,
While you and I, dilly, dilly,
Keep ourselves warm.

Mary, Mary, quite contrary,
How does your garden grow?
With silver bells, and cockle shells,
And pretty maids all in a row!

I had a little nut tree,
Nothing would it bear
But a silver nutmeg
And a golden pear.

The King of Spain's daughter
Came to visit me,
And all for the sake
Of my little nut tree.

The Queen of Hearts
She made some tarts,
All on a summer's day;
The Knave of Hearts
He stole the tarts,
And took them right away.

The King of Hearts
Called for the tarts,
And beat the Knave full sore;
The Knave of Hearts
Brought back the tarts,
And vowed he'd steal no more.

58

ACTION
RHYMES

Round and round the garden
Like a teddy bear.
One step, two steps,
Tickle you under there!

Teddy bear, teddy bear,
Turn around.
Teddy bear, teddy bear,
Touch the ground.

Teddy bear, teddy bear,
Climb the stairs.
Teddy bear, teddy bear,
Say your prayers.

Teddy bear, teddy bear,
Turn out the light.
Teddy bear, teddy bear,
Say good night.

60

One, two, three, four, five,
Once I caught a fish alive.
Six, seven, eight, nine, ten,
Then I let it go again.

Why did you let it go?
Because it bit my finger so.
Which finger did it bite?
This little finger on the right.

Tinker,
Tailor,
Soldier,
Sailor,
Rich man,
Poor man,
Beggar man,
Thief.

61

One, two,
Buckle my shoe;

Three, four,
Knock on the door;

Five, six,
Pick up sticks;

Seven, eight,
Lay them straight;

Nine, ten,
My fat hen;

Eleven, twelve,
Dig and delve;

Thirteen, fourteen,
Maids a-courting;

Fifteen, sixteen,
Maids in the kitchen;

Seventeen, eighteen,
Maids in waiting;

Nineteen, twenty,
My plate's empty.

This little pig
went to market,

This little pig
stayed at home.

This little pig
had roast beef,

This little pig
had none.

And this little pig
cried, "Wee-wee-wee!"
All the way home.

As I was going to St. Ives,
I met a man with seven wives.
Each wife had seven sacks,
Each sack had seven cats,
Each cat had seven kits.
Kits, cats, sacks and wives,
How many were going to St. Ives?

Incey, wincey spider,
Climbing up the spout,
Along came the rain
And washed the spider out!

Pat-a-cake, pat-a-cake, baker's man,
Bake me a cake as fast as you can;
Pat it and prick it and mark it with B,
Put it in the oven for baby and me.

Oranges and lemons,
Say the bells of St. Clement's.

You owe me five farthings,
Say the bells of St. Martin's.

When will you pay me?
Say the bells of Old Bailey.

When I grow rich,
Say the bells of Shoreditch.

When will that be?
Say the bells of Stepney.

I'm sure I don't know,
Says the great bell of Bow.

Here comes a candle
To light you to bed.
And here comes a chopper
To chop off your head!

London Bridge is falling down,
Falling down, falling down,
London Bridge is falling down,
    My fair lady.

Build it up with wood and clay,
Wood and clay, wood and clay,
Build it up with wood and clay,
    My fair lady.

Wood and clay will wash away,
Wash away, wash away,
Wood and clay will wash away,
    My fair lady.

Build it up with bricks and mortar,
Bricks and mortar, bricks and mortar,
Build it up with bricks and mortar,
    My fair lady.

Ring-a-ring o' roses,
A pocket full of posies.
A-tish-oo! A-tish-oo!
We all fall down!

Dance to your Daddy,
My little laddie,
Dance to your Daddy,
My little lamb!
You shall have a fishy
On a little dishy,
You shall have a fishy
When the boat comes in.

Dance to your Daddy,
My little laddie,
Dance to your Daddy,
My little lamb!
You shall have an apple,
You shall have a plum,
You shall have a rattle-basket,
When your Dad comes home.

68

BEDTIME RHYMES

Wee Willie Winkie runs
through the town,
Upstairs and downstairs
in his nightgown.
Rapping at the window,
Crying through the lock,
"Are all the children in their beds?
It's past eight o'clock!"

How many miles to Babylon?
Three score miles and ten.
Can I get there by candlelight?
Yes, and back again.
If your heels are nimble and light,
You may get there by candlelight.

Jack, be nimble,
Jack, be quick,
Jack, jump over the candlestick!

Sleep, baby, sleep,
Thy father guards the sheep,
Thy mother shakes
    the dreamland tree,
And from it fall
    sweet dreams for thee.
Sleep, baby, sleep.

Sleep, baby, sleep,
Our cottage vale is deep.
The little lamb is on the green,
With woolly fleece so soft and clean.
Sleep, baby, sleep.

Sleep, baby, sleep,
Down where the woodbines creep,
Be always like the lamb so mild,
A kind and sweet and gentle child.
Sleep, baby, sleep.

Rock-a-bye, baby, rock, rock, rock,
Baby shall have a new pink frock!
A new pink frock and a ribbon to tie,
If baby is good and does not cry.

Rock-a-bye, baby, rock, rock, rock,
Listen, who comes
        with a knock, knock, knock?
Oh, it is pussy! Come in, come in!
Mother and baby are always at home.

Diddle, diddle, dumpling,
        my son John,
Went to bed with his trousers on!
One shoe off and one shoe on,
Diddle, diddle, dumpling,
        my son John.

Twinkle, twinkle, little star,
How I wonder what you are!
Up above the world so high,
Like a diamond in the sky,
Twinkle, twinkle, little star,
How I wonder what you are!

When the blazing sun is gone,
When he nothing shines upon,
Then you show your little light,
Twinkle, twinkle, all the night.

In the dark blue sky you keep,
And often through my curtains peep,
For you never shut your eye,
Till the sun is in the sky.

Star light, star bright,
First star I see tonight,
I wish I may, I wish I might,
Have the wish I wish tonight.

I see the moon,
And the moon sees me.
God bless the moon,
And God bless me.

The man in the moon
Came down too soon
And asked the way to Norwich;
He went by the south
And burned his mouth
By eating cold plum porridge.

Hush, little baby, don't say a word,
Papa's going to buy you
    a mockingbird.

If that mockingbird won't sing,
Papa's going to buy you
    a diamond ring.

If that diamond ring turns brass,
Papa's going to buy you
    a looking glass.

If that looking glass gets broke,
Papa's going to buy you
    a billy goat.

If that billy goat won't pull,
Papa's going to buy you
    a cart and bull.

76

If that cart and bull turns over,
Papa's going to buy you
    a dog named Rover.

If that dog named Rover won't bark,
Papa's going to buy you
    a horse and cart.

If that horse and cart fall down,
You'll still be the sweetest little baby
    in town.

Hush-a-bye, don't you cry,
Go to sleep little baby,
When you wake, you shall have
All the pretty little horses.
Blacks and bays, dapples and greys,
Coach and six little horses.

Hush-a-bye, baby,
On the treetop,
When the wind blows,
The cradle will rock.
When the bough breaks,
The cradle will fall,
And down will come baby,
Cradle and all.

Good night,
Sleep tight,
Wake up bright
In the morning light
To do what's right
With all your might.

INDEX